BAA

by Shauna Arnold
illustrated by Irene Hines

Written for my daughter, Kaylee.

Trinity Books
Cascade, Idaho

Published in the United States by Trinity Books.
Printed in the United States of America
First Edition

ISBN: 0-9743669-0-0
Library of Congress Catalog Number: 2003096025

Baa is a floppy tumble bean bag lamb ("LuLu" - item # 10212) - a product of
Fiesta and manufactured by Fiesta.

Trinity Books
P.O. Box 401
Cascade, Idaho 83611

The story of "Baa" was inspired by my daughter, Kaylee, and her special friend, "Baa" - a stuffed lamb. When Kaylee became lost in a toy store, she found security in her newfound friend. They became inseparable, and this story represents some of their adventures together.

Special thanks to my mom and Shelley Metzger for their support and proofreading abilities, my dad for his encouragement, Sue Anderson for helping make the story come alive, and Matt Miller for his graphic design assistance.

Hi! My name is Baa.
This is my best friend, Kaylee.

We have been friends
for as long as I can
remember.

One day, long ago, I met Kaylee in the big toy store where I used to live. Kaylee's grandma had taken her there. It turned out to be my lucky day and the beginning of a great friendship.

Kaylee wandered off to look at the stuffed
animals. I was sitting on a low shelf next
to Pokey Bear, Pongo Puppy, and Rosy Rabbit.
Kaylee picked me out of all the others. She
gave me a big hug, and I just knew I would be
going home with her!

Kaylee said, "Grandma might be worried about us, Baa. Maybe we should sit in this little rocking chair so she can find us."

We settled into the rocking chair, and Kaylee rocked me back and forth, back and forth.

Kaylee's grandma came around the aisle where the bright-yellow toy trucks sat on the floor. She looked very happy to see Kaylee and me. We were safe and waiting for her to take us home.

Kaylee takes me everywhere.
We have so many fun adventures!

My favorite was the
time she took me to
the ocean.

6

We played tag with the big ocean waves that came crashing up on the shore.

We built tall sandcastles that Kaylee's little brother toppled over with one quick swipe of his hands.

"Look, Baa," Kaylee squealed, "that seal is playing hide-and-seek with us!"

8

Mr. Seal poked his shiny head out of the water and looked at us with a watery smile.

Kaylee and I giggled. We watched him bob in and out of the water like a cork, showing us how well he could swim.

Big whales also came up from the deep, blue ocean. They squirted water from their spouts - high into the air like a gigantic water fountain at the park.

Kaylee and I loved our ocean adventure!

Back when I was new, I had a beautiful, fluffy coat of wool, but Kaylee likes to tickle me. She pulls and tugs on my coat until little pieces of "linty-Baa" cover our car and house.

Kaylee's mom says it looks like it is snowing inside whenever we play!

Now I have bare patches where my wool is missing. I don't mind if my coat is no longer beautiful or fluffy and neither does Kaylee.

She still takes good care of me and keeps me warm with snuggly hugs and lovey kisses.

One day, Kaylee's mom said, "Baa, we need to give you a bath!" Since my coat was no longer white and fluffy, I agreed.

Kaylee's mom placed me in a round container that had a large window.

I could see Kaylee standing outside the window looking at me as I rolled around in the warm, sudsy water.

Kaylee had tears in her eyes and looked sad. I tried to let her know everything was okay. I winked at her to show her I wasn't afraid.

Kaylee's mom then placed me in another round container. This one didn't have a window, but it sure was warm inside!

I spun around and around. A buzzer beeped, and I was dry and clean!

Kaylee hugged me tight and said,
"Oh, I missed you, Baa!"

She told me I was
nice, white, and fluffy
again.

Every night Kaylee snuggles with her mom in the big rocking chair. Of course, I am right there with them.

This is my favorite time of the day!

Kaylee's mom reads our favorite stories to us until we fall fast asleep.

I am wrapped in my best friend's arms, and I dream about all the fun we'll have when we wake in the morning light.

The End